THE LOVELY SUMMER

The Lovely Summer

by
Marc Simont

A BANTAM LITTLE ROOSTER BOOK
NEW YORK · TORONTO · LONDON · SYDNEY · AUCKLAND

The Lovely Summer is grateful to the lovely Sally Doherty
for her patience and good judgment
—M.S.

THE LOVELY SUMMER

A Bantam Little Rooster Book/April 1992

*Little Rooster is a trademark of Bantam Books, a division of
Bantam Doubleday Dell Publishing Group, Inc.*

For information address: Bantam Books.

Library of Congress Cataloging-in-Publication Data
Simont, Marc.
The lovely summer / by Marc Simont.
p.   cm.
"A Bantam little rooster book."
*Summary: Gladys and Jerome, two cottontail rabbits,
outsmart the owners of a vegetable garden.*
ISBN 0-553-07716-3
[1. Rabbits—Fiction. 2. Gardens—Fiction.]   I. Title.
PZ7.S6058Lo   1992
[E]—dc20   90-29324
CIP
AC

Published simultaneously in the United States and Canada

*Bantam Books are published by Bantam Books, a division of Bantam Doubleday Dell Publishing Group,
Inc. Its trademark, consisting of the words "Bantam Books" and the portrayal of a rooster, is Registered
in U.S. Patent and Trademark Office and in other countries. Marca Registrada. Bantam Books, 666 Fifth
Avenue, New York, New York 10103.*

PRINTED IN HONG KONG

SCP   0 9 8 7 6 5 4 3 2 1

For Doc

Gladys and Jerome were cottontail rabbits. Hopping through the woods with their children one day, they came upon a clearing.

"Look!" said Gladys. "People!"

A man and a woman were digging in the dirt. A small dog was asleep nearby.

Jerome eyed them suspiciously.

"I wonder what they're up to," he whispered.

The people looked up from their vegetable garden and saw the rabbits.

The little dog woke up and barked.

"Time to go!" said Jerome, and they ran back into the woods.

"Why do we always run from people?" Gladys asked.

Jerome was surprised at the question. "Because we're shy," he explained. "All rabbits are shy."

The next time the rabbits came to the clearing, there was a fence around the garden.

"What a pretty fence!" Gladys said.

Jerome was busy digging and he didn't hear.

The garden was filled with wonderful things to eat.

"Eat the spinach, children," said Gladys. "It's very good for you."

"Hey," called Jerome, "looka yonder."

There, glaring at them through the fence, stood Globby, the woodchuck.

"That pest," said Gladys. "Thank goodness for the fence!"

Suddenly the little dog came yapping at Globby and
chased him away.

"Such a good little dog," Gladys said.

Then the people came and made a fuss.

"Time to go!" said Jerome.

Sometime later the rabbits were surprised to find a large
box in the garden.
"What's that?" Jerome wanted to know.

"It looks like a little house," answered Gladys. "Do you suppose they want us to live here?" she wondered.
"Not so fast," warned Jerome. "It could be a trap."
"Don't be ridiculous," said Gladys. Then she saw the carrot inside the box. "Look!" she said. "The nice people even set out breakfast for us."

"Beat it!"

The rabbits froze in their tracks.

"Globby!" they gasped.

"You heard me," Globby snarled. "Out!"

"This is not for you, Globby," said Gladys bravely.

"This is *our* garden," Jerome added.

"BEAT IT!" Globby said again. He took a step toward them. Globby was big.

"Time to go!" said Jerome, leading a hasty retreat back to the woods.

Globby looked around the garden and gloated. "It's all mine," he said.

Then he saw the carrot. "I think I'll start here." But just as he bit the carrot—WHAM!—the trapdoor slammed shut. Globby was caught.

At dusk, the people came and took the box away.

By the time the rabbits felt it was safe to return, the garden was in its full midsummer splendor.
"Where's Gwobby?" asked one of the little ones.
But there were no signs of Globby anywhere.

"The garden is beautiful!" Gladys exclaimed, and the
rabbits settled down to their feast.
"Such nice people," Gladys observed. "They even pulled
up the weeds."
"Yeah," said Jerome, "and left us the good stuff."

When the people arrived to weed the garden, they
seemed upset.
The little dog started barking.
"Time to go," said Jerome,
and the rabbits knew what to do.

Early one morning, the man took a gun and headed for the garden.
Squinting through the morning mist he saw what looked like a rabbit behind a tomato plant.

"What was that?" Jerome asked.
"Let's go and find out," said Gladys. Rabbits may be shy,
but they're also curious.

When they got there, the man was walking away, gun in one hand, leaky can in the other.

"Why did the man do that, Daddy?" asked one of the children.

Jerome thought for a moment. "People do strange things," he said.

Days went by. The rabbits spent nearly all their time in the garden.
The people hardly ever came. They didn't even weed it.
One frosty morning the people put suitcases in the car, locked up the cottage, and started off.

As they drove past the garden, the man leaned out the
window and shook his fist at the rabbits.

"Look," said Gladys, "the nice man is waving to us. Wave
back, everybody."

The rabbits kept waving as the car went down the lane,
turned the corner, and was gone.

"I hope those nice people come back next year," said
Jerome.
"Me, too," said Gladys. "They were so good to us.
It's been a lovely summer."